A GREAT DAY for *PUP*

Climb in, Dick and Sally.
It is time now to go
to wherever on earth
the wild babies grow.

The Cat in the Hat's Learning Library®
introduces beginning readers to basic non-
fiction. If your child can read these lines,
then he or she can begin to understand the
fascinating world in which we live.

Learn to read. Read to learn.

*For a list of books in **The Cat in the Hat's Learning Library**, see the back endpaper.*

The editors would like to thank
BARBARA KIEFER, Ph.D.,
Charlotte S. Huck Professor of Children's Literature,
The Ohio State University, and
JIM BREHENY,
Director, Bronx Zoo,
for their assistance in the preparation of this book.

Visit us on the Web!
www.randomhouse.com/kids
Seussville.com

Educators and librarians, for a variety of teaching tools, visit us at www.randomhouse.com/teachers

Library of Congress Cataloging-in-Publication Data
Worth, Bonnie.
A great day for pup : all about wild babies / by Bonnie Worth ; illustrated by Aristides Ruiz.
  p. cm. — (The Cat in the Hat's learning library)
Summary: The Cat in the Hat introduces Dick and Sally to various animal babies in the wild.
ISBN 978-0-375-81096-1 (trade) — ISBN 978-0-375-91096-8 (lib. bdg.)
[1. Animals—Infancy—Fiction. 2. Stories in rhyme.] I. Ruiz, Aristides, ill. II. Title. III. Series.
PZ8.3.W896 Gr 2002 [E]—dc21 2001031624

Printed in the United States of America
16 15 14 13 12 11 ·10 9 8 7 6

A GREAT DAY for PUP

by Bonnie Worth

illustrated by Aristides Ruiz

The Cat in the Hat's Learning Library™

Random House 🏠 New York

It's a great day for pup
and for joey and calf.
A great day to learn.
A great day to laugh.

I have fixed up a jeep
that could not be sweeter.
It's my Super-de-Duper
Wild Animal Greeter!

6

Climb in, Dick and Sally.
It is time now to go
to wherever on earth
the wild babies grow.

The motor is racing!
And it is no wonder.
We have a long trip to . . .

. . . Australia—down under!

Ma Kangaroo's pouch
is safe as a purse.
It's where her joey
will grow and will nurse

8

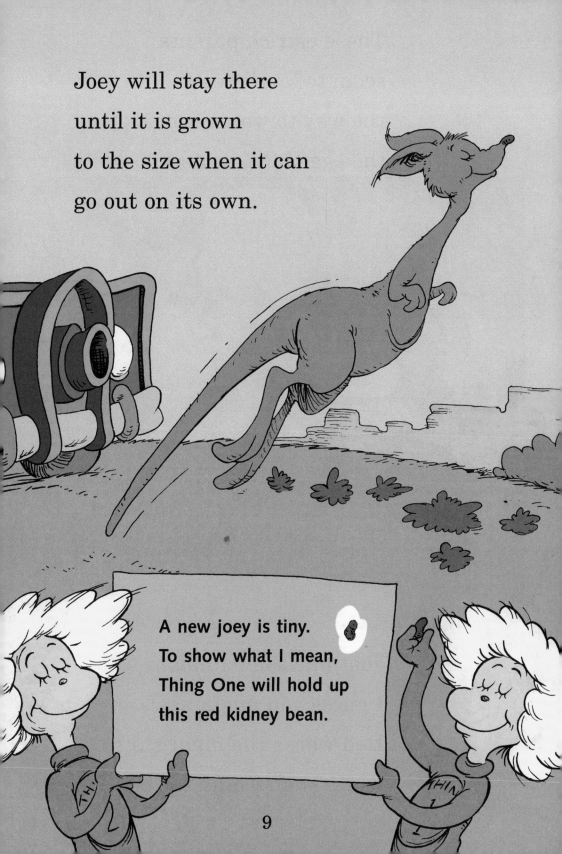

Joey will stay there
until it is grown
to the size when it can
go out on its own.

A new joey is tiny.
To show what I mean,
Thing One will hold up
this red kidney bean.

These ostrich parents
seem to know best
the way to watch over
the eggs in their nest.

Just like some humans,
I guess you might say:
Dad works the night shift,
while Mom works the day.

When the chicks hatch,
they get up and go
off to learn lessons.
They march in a row.

Intro to Bug Hunting.
Plants to Eat 101.
The chicks learn to kick
and they learn how to run.

When a predator comes,

Dad knows just what to do.

He runs in zigzags, flaps

his wings, and says BOOO-OOO!

What is a predator?
I hear you ask me.
A predator's a
natural enemy!

And here is a mom who
might give you a shock
with her rows of sharp teeth.
Yes, this mom is a croc!

For seventy days,
she watches her nest.
She even stops eating!
Won't take time to rest!

The baby crocs hatch
while under the ground.
Their mom digs them up
when they let out this sound.
UH! UH!

Then she opens up **wide**,
lets them all crawl inside,
and at the bank of the river
they take their first ride.

And now for more babies
to really amaze ya,
we'll journey up north . . .

. . . to the forests of Asia!

Here, Panda Mom gives her cub sweet loving care. She has to. It's blind— and has almost no hair!

She feeds her cub milk
and she cuddles it tight.
For months, she won't let
that cub out of her sight.

Thing One has a chart
on which he will show
just how fast this cute
panda baby will grow.

At one month, the baby
can't do much at all.
At four months, it is
just beginning to crawl.

At seven months, it
can climb and can chew
on the fast-growing plant
that we know as bamboo.

For three years, this tigress
watches over her brood.
She keeps them all warm and
she hunts down their food.

She teaches it how to
stay cool and survive—
where the mud wallows are,
where the tasty plants thrive.

When the elephant mom
finds her job a bit smothering,
a young gal helps out.
This is called allomothering.

We'll leave Asia now,
for it's getting later,
and travel to Africa
below the equator.

How many babies
do we have on hand
in this troop of gorillas,
who live in a band?
Three baby gorillas,
who get lots of hugs.
Their moms groom their fur
and check them for bugs.

The troop likes to move,
but when baby needs rest,
the mother gorilla
will build it a nest.

And look over there!
Why, it's Mother Giraffe.
And she's just given birth
to a cute giraffe calf.

Already he's standing!
When he wants to eat,
he will open up wide
and let out a bleat.

30

You'll never believe this,
but I have been told:
giraffes go to kindergarten
at just two weeks old!

And what have we here?
A zebra colt—yipes!
But where did it get
all those brown stripes?

32

The stripes turn black later.
Now it must run fast.
If a colt cannot run,
a colt will not last.

Now we are going
to where it is cold
to visit some chicks who
are just two weeks old.

This baby king penguin
looks ever so sweet,
cuddled all cozy
between Daddy's feet.

The chicks want to eat.

They want to eat now.

(In an hour, they eat

over two pounds of chow!)

Here's a polar bear fact that
I think you should know:
cubs are born in a den
deep under the snow!

At three months of age,

they all squeeze outside,

where the cubs like to romp

and tumble and slide.

It's a great day for pup
and her sea lion mother.
But Mom and her pup
are so far from each other!

They bark back and forth.
They are really quite loud.
And that way the pup
won't get lost in the crowd.

38

It's time to go now.

It's time to say bye.

Please don't be sad, Sally.

Oh, Dick, please don't cry.

I will fix up your backyard.

I will do it for you.

Your mother will not
mind at all if I do.

So, please take my hand.

It is time now to enter

your very own

wild baby . . .

... DAY-CARE CENTER!

GLOSSARY

Allomother: A female animal who helps a mother care for her young.

Bleat: An animal noise that sounds like a sad cry.

Brood: A group of young born or hatched at the same time.

Crude: Raw or blunt and lacking in smoothness.

Den: The lair or shelter of a wild animal.

Down under: A term often used to describe Australia because it is "down under" the equator.

Equator: A circle around the Earth that is an equal distance between the North and South Poles.

Groom: To clean by removing dirt or parasites from the fur, skin, feathers, etc.

Joey: A young animal, usually a kangaroo.

Kindergarten: A group of young giraffes, usually cared for briefly by a single female giraffe.

Predator: An animal that hunts and catches other animals for food.

Prey: An animal hunted or caught for food.

Thrive: To grow quickly and well; flourish.

Troop: A group of animals, usually primates.

Wallow: A dusty or muddy place where wild animals go to roll around in order to cool down or make themselves comfortable.

FOR FURTHER READING

Baby Animals by Andrew Brown (Crabtree, *Extraordinary Animals* series). Facts about amazing baby animals such as kangaroos, fruit bats, and cheetahs. For grades 1 and up.

I Wonder Why Kangaroos Have Pouches and Other Questions About Baby Animals by Jenny Wood (Kingfisher, *I Wonder Why* series). Answers questions about baby animals such as "Why do birds turn their eggs?" and "Which is the biggest baby animal?" For preschoolers and up.

Safe, Warm, and Snug by Stephen R. Swinburne, illustrated by Jose Aruego and Ariane Dewey (Gulliver Books). A collection of poems that explain the ways different animals protect their babies. For preschoolers and up.

Wild Babies by Seymour Simon (HarperTrophy). All about the growth and care of such youngsters as baby elephants, dolphins, and alligators. For kindergarten and up.

INDEX